07A

THIS BOOK BELONGS TO:

_____

30131 05387124 7

LONDON BOROUGH OF BARNET

To my Sóley,
may you always follow your feet to magical places

First published in Great Britain in 2016 by Andersen Press Ltd.,
20 Vauxhall Bridge Road, London SW1V 2SA.

Originally published by Alfred A. Knopf, an imprint of Random House Children's Books,
a division of Penguin Random House LLC, New York.

Copyright © Alfred A. Knopf
Copyright © Birgitta Sif, 2016

The right of Birgitta Sif to be identified as the author and illustrator of this work
have been asserted by her in accordance with the Copyrights, Designs and Patents Act, 1988.

All rights reserved.

Printed in China.

1 3 5 7 9 10 8 6 4 2

British Library Cataloguing in Information Data available.

ISBN 978 1 78344 363 5

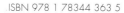

WHERE MY FEET GO

BIRGITTA SIF

ANDERSEN PRESS

Do you know where my feet go in the morning?

One green sock,

one purple sock,

two yellow

moon boots...

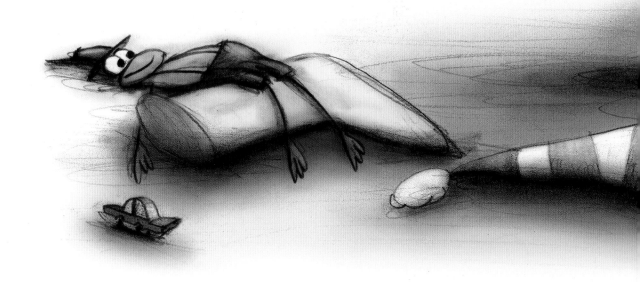

then straight out the door!

But my feet don't walk
a normal walk,
down a normal street...

My feet go trampling
through the thick jungle.

My feet go climbing
over tall mountains.

My feet go tiptoeing
across a
creaking bridge.

And my feet
go splashing in
the sea.

What about in
the afternoon?
Do you know where
my feet go then?

My feet sit very, very quietly
while I feed little dinosaurs.

Then my feet go higher and higher.

My feet get tickled by the clouds.

Wait just one second...
where did my feet go?

There my feet go!

Shuffling through the desert,
looking for a spot to build a castle!

Do you know where
my feet go at night?

Before bed, my feet go underwater exploring.

My feet go flying
to the moon!

So, where do you
want to go next?

I think my feet
will go to some very
magical places...